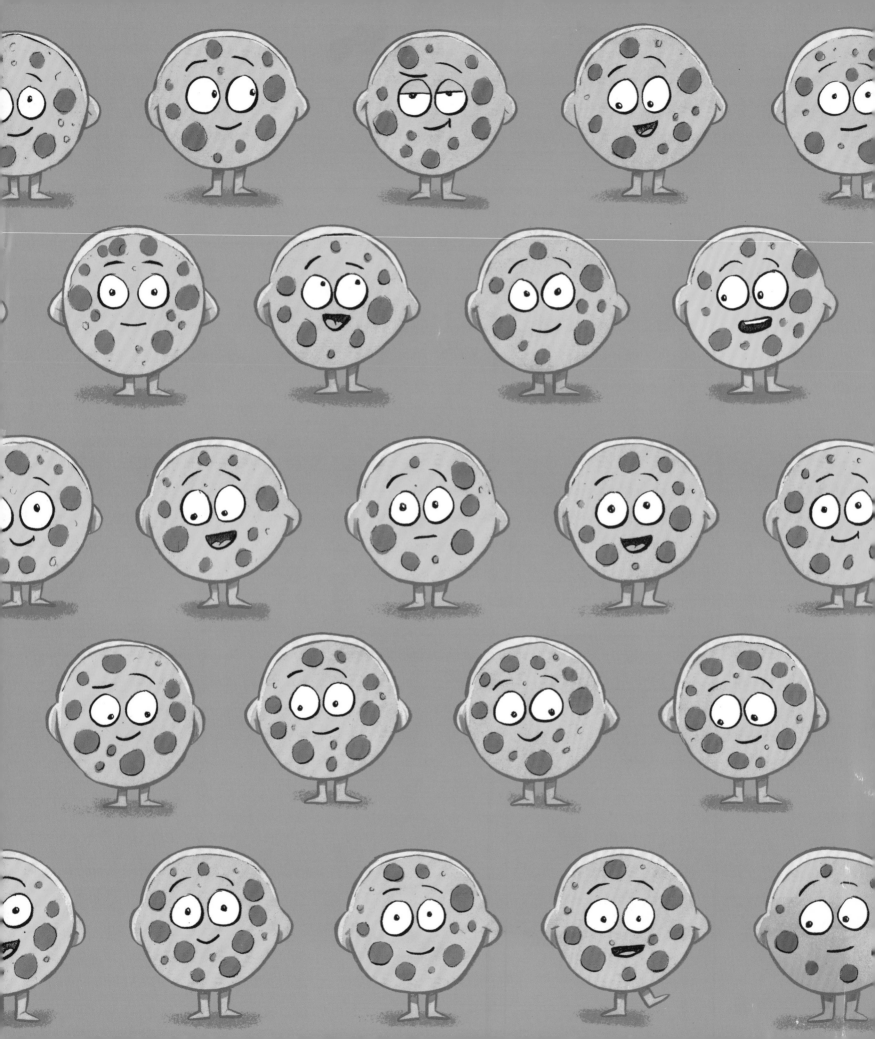

For Michael Ashton,
the best kind
of cookie. MR

For Jodie Smith. TK

WHEN COOKIE CRUMBLED

MICHELLE ROBINSON & TOM KNIGHT

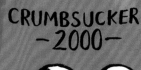

CRUMBSUCKER
—2000—

SCHOLASTIC

NO SUPRISES
COOKIES

NICE N' SIMPLE
COOKIES

NICE N' SIM
COOKIE

NO SU
COO

NO SUPRI
COOKI

Every cookie in the batch looked
pretty much the same.
You couldn't tell them all apart,
so they all shared one name.

She was Cookie.

He was Cookie.

They were Cookie. See?

With everyone the same it made life simple as can be.

But somebody was running late . . .
the others looked appalled.

Michael didn't look like all his sisters and his brothers.
He wasn't nice and round, or beige and spotty, like the others.

So, Michael shook his sprinkles off and got back in the batch.

The next day, all the little cookies lined up in a row.
"Where is Michael?" Cookie said.
"Does anybody know?"

"Here I am!" said Michael,
"Sorry I'm a little late.
I had to put these sweeties on.
I love them, aren't they great?"

At roll call the next morning,
he tried *just* a hint of spice.
Not only did it look a **treat**
but, wow, did he smell **nice**!

Michael asked, "Would *you* like some?"
The others groaned and grumbled.

AACHOO!

They shook their heads and tutted,
then they muttered and they mumbled.

"Fall in line,"
they said to him.
"Be plain! Be good! Be neat!
Be what cookies *should be* —
super round and super sweet."

He spent his day the boring way, the same as all the rest.
But being individual's what Michael loved the best.

"Plain and spotty's fine,
but it just isn't who I am.
I really need a splash of chocolate sauce
or strawberry jam . . ."

He tried some on.

Oh,
goodness!

All the cookies gasped in shock.
Their constant disapproval
gave his confidence a knock.

His heart was close to breaking as
he climbed back on the shelf.

"*Everyone* has differences.
Why can't I be myself?"

He tried it
one last time.

Too weird.

Too much.

Too different.

Ta-daa!

Now tell me what you think!

Too disgusting.

FAR TOO PINK!

Should he be like all the rest?

His feelings were so jumbled!

He'd **never** felt so all alone . . .

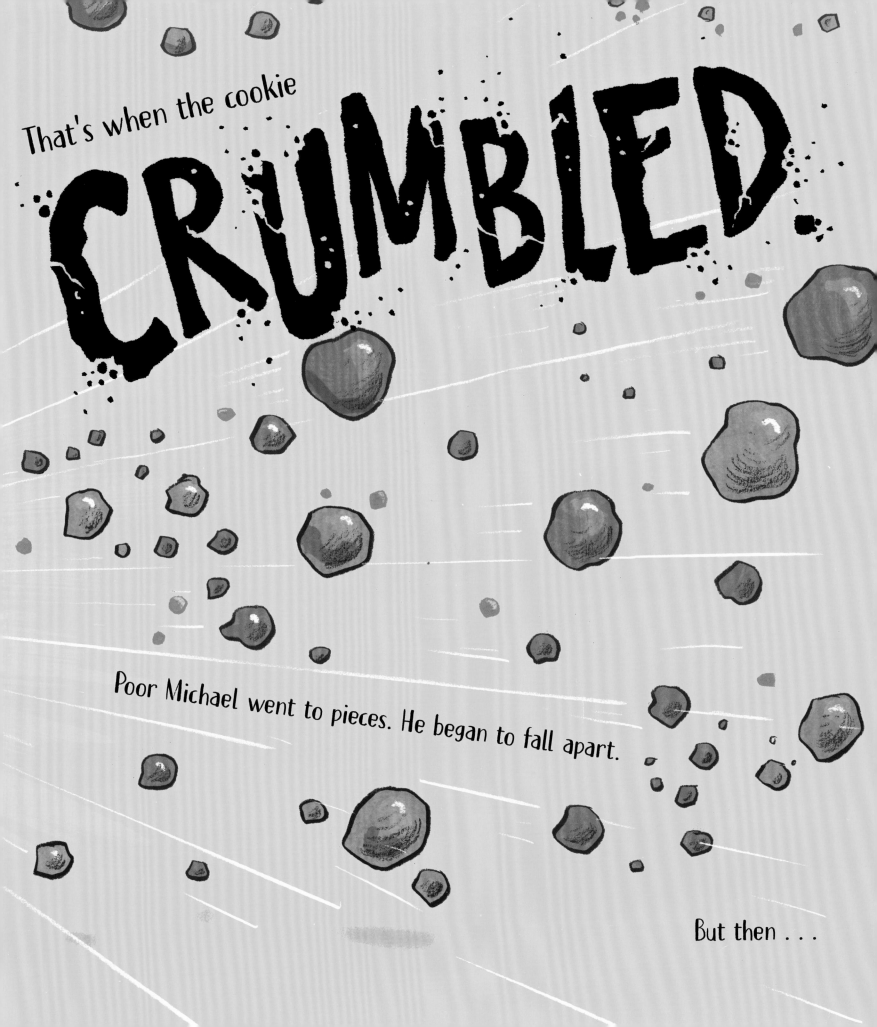

That's when the cookie

CRUMBLED

Poor Michael went to pieces. He began to fall apart.

But then . . .

. . . he took a big, deep breath
and listened to his heart.

Michael stood up tall and strong.
"Why *shouldn't* I look square?

Who *cares* if I have fancy bits and icing everywhere?"

Now, Michael didn't mean to squeeze the icing tube so tight . . .
But, too late! Blobs of icing had already taken flight.
The cookies got a coating as it rained down on the floor!

Michael thought they'd all be cross, but they called out for . . .

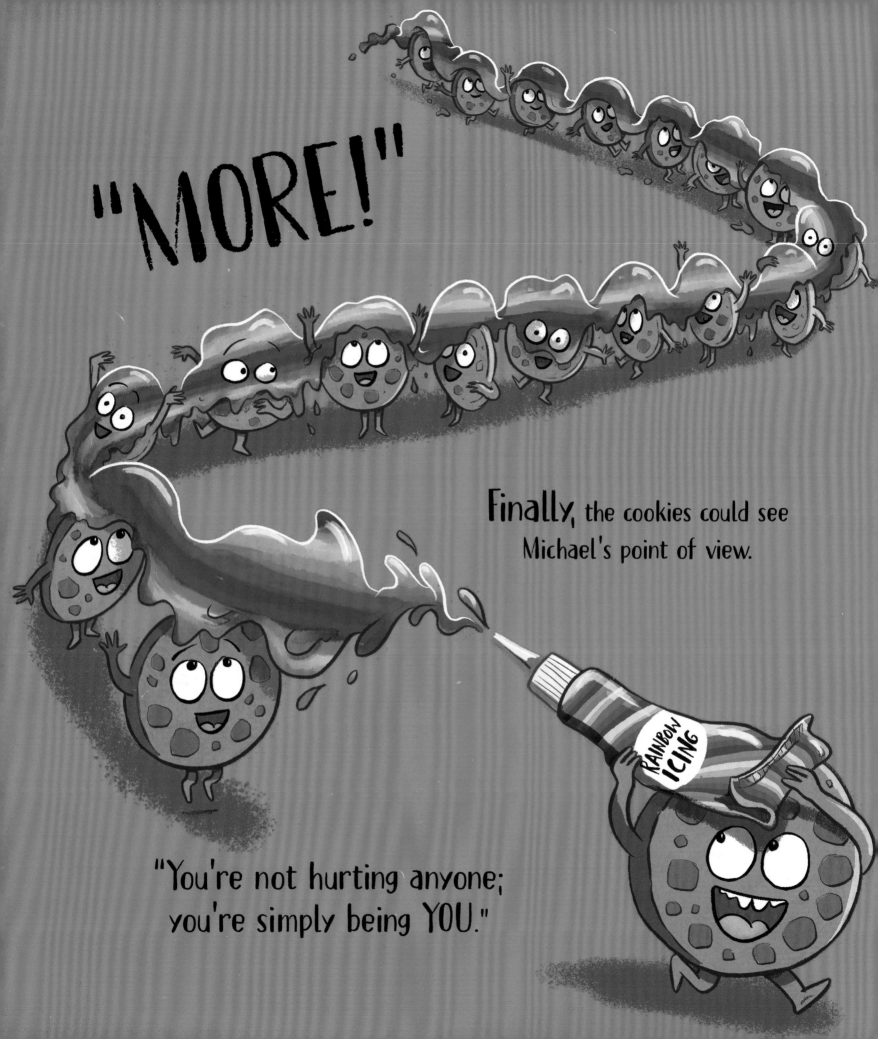

"MORE!"

Finally, the cookies could see Michael's point of view.

"You're not hurting anyone; you're simply being YOU."

They came out of their packets and they jumped down off the shelves.

"You are one **smart** cookie!

It feels **good** to be ourselves!"

They danced the whole night long,
with no more lining up in rows.
They shook off all their worries
and they put on
what they chose.

Now Michael and his cookie friends
no longer really match.
So what if they're all different?

They're one great big, happy batch!

Published in the UK by Scholastic, 2023
1 London Bridge, London, SE1 9BG
Scholastic Ireland, 89E Lagan Road, Dublin Industrial Estate, Glasnevin, Dublin, D11 HP5F

SCHOLASTIC and associated logos are trademarks and/or registered trademarks of Scholastic Inc.

Text © Michelle Robinson, 2023
Illustrations © Tom Knight, 2023

The right of Michelle Robinson and Tom Knight to be identified as the author and illustrator of this work
has been asserted by them under the Copyright, Designs and Patents Act 1988.

ISBN 978 0702 32485 7

A CIP catalogue record for this book is available from the British Library.

Printed in Italy
Paper made from wood grown in sustainable forests and other controlled sources.
1 3 5 7 9 10 8 6 4 2

This is a work of fiction. Names, characters, places, incidents and dialogues are products of the author's imagination
or are used fictitiously. Any resemblance to actual people, living or dead, events or locales is entirely coincidental.

www.scholastic.co.uk

FSC
www.fsc.org
MIXT
Paper | Donant
suport a la
silvicultura
responsable
FSC® C023419